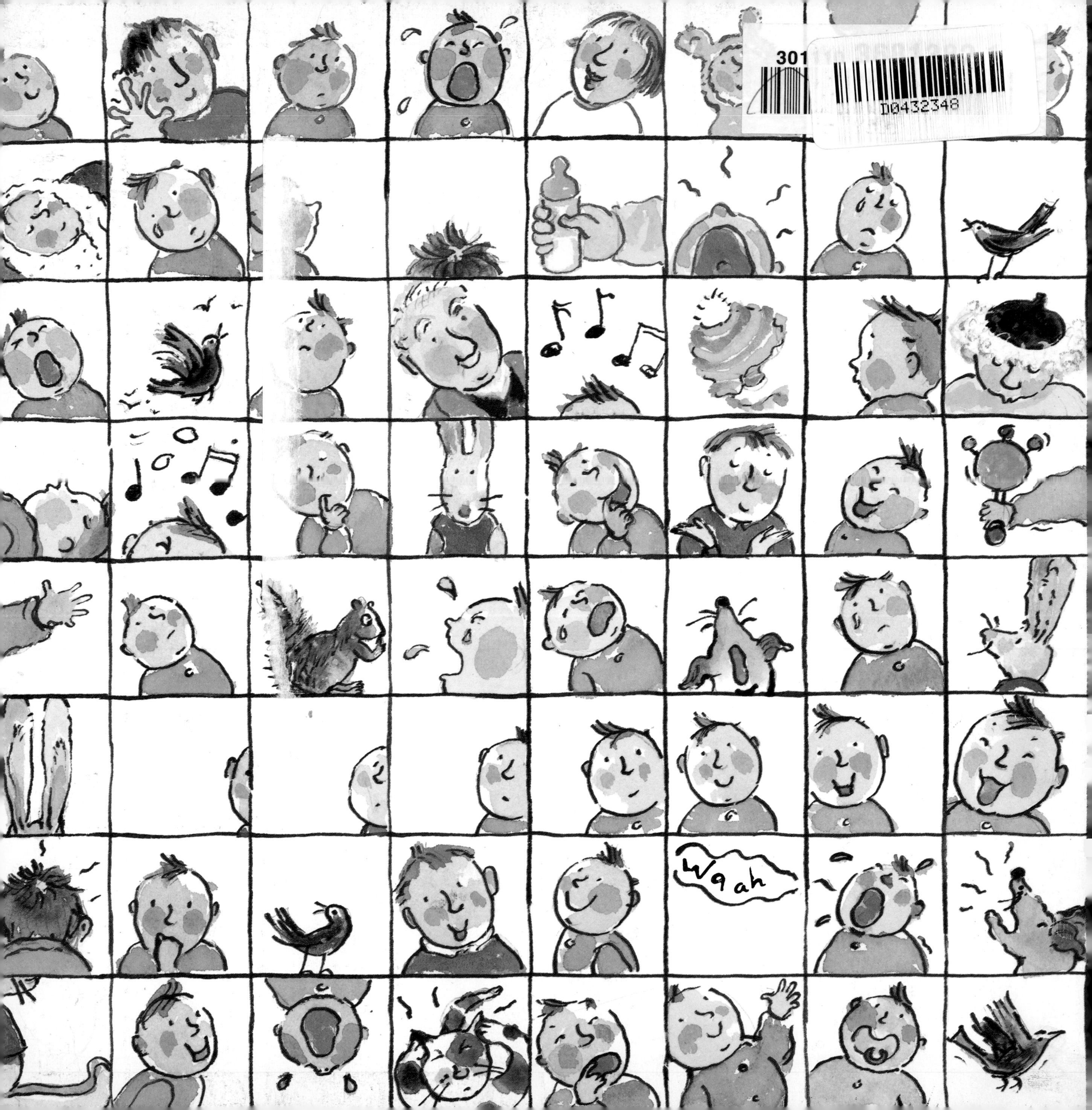
Waah

To David and Suzie, who share something special.
F.W.
For Clare and Chloë.
C.T.

TRANSWORLD PUBLISHERS LTD
61-63 Uxbridge Road, London W5 5SA

TRANSWORLD PUBLISHERS (AUSTRALIA) PTY LTD
15-25 Helles Avenue, Moorebank, NSW 2170

TRANSWORLD PUBLISHERS (NZ) LTD
3 William Pickering Drive, Albany, Auckland

DOUBLEDAY CANADA LTD
105 Bond Street, Toronto, Ontario M5B 1Y3

Published in 1998 by Doubleday
a division of Transworld Publishers Ltd

Designed by Ian Butterworth

A catalogue record for this book is available from the British Library

ISBN 0 385 409451

Printed in Italy

Oonga Boonga

Frieda Wishinsky · Carol Thompson

DOUBLEDAY
London · New York · Toronto · Sydney · Auckland

Nobody could make
Baby Louise stop crying.

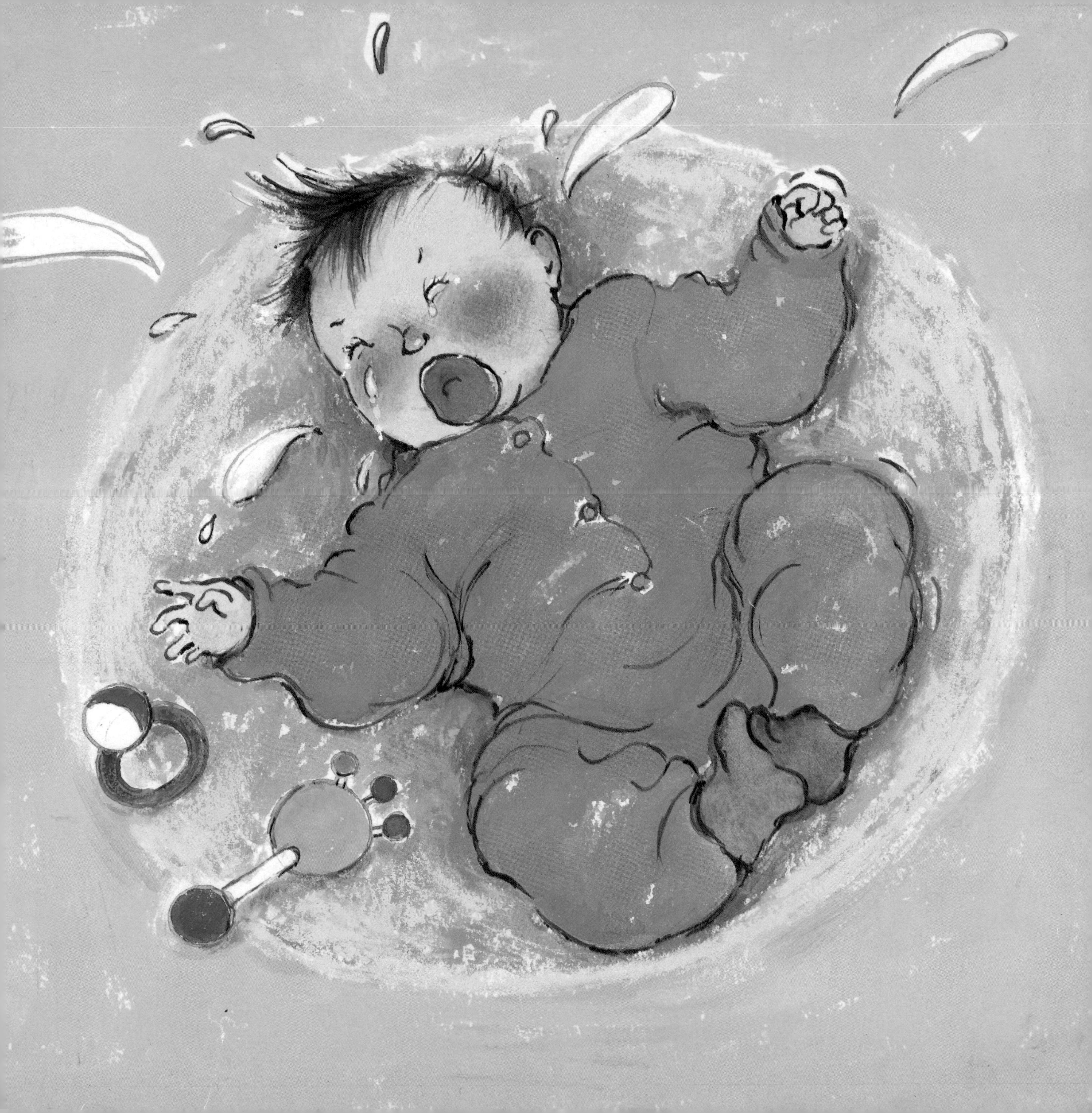

Her mother tried.

She held her close and sang a little lullaby.

But that didn't help.

Louise kept on crying till her tears ran

like rivers to the sea.

Her father tried.

He rocked her gently in his arms
and whispered softly in her ear.
But that didn't help.
Louise kept on crying till her wails
shook the pictures off the walls.

Grandma tried.

She gave her a nice warm bottle

and said, “Drink, baby. Drink.”

But that didn’t help.

Louise kept on crying till her sobs woke all the

dogs and cats on the block.

Grandpa tried.

He played a happy tune on his harmonica and did a little jig.

But that didn't help.

Louise kept on crying till the birds flew out of the trees and the squirrels scampered away.

The neighbours came and offered advice.

"Turn her on her stomach." "Turn her on her side."

"Play Mozart." "Play rock and roll."

But nothing helped. Louise kept on crying.

Then, her brother Daniel came home from school.

"OONGA BOONGA," he said to Louise.

Louise looked up, tears streaming down her face.

"OONGA BOONGA," he repeated.

Louise stopped sobbing and looked him straight in the eye.

"OONGA BOONGA," said Daniel again.

Louise broke into a smile.

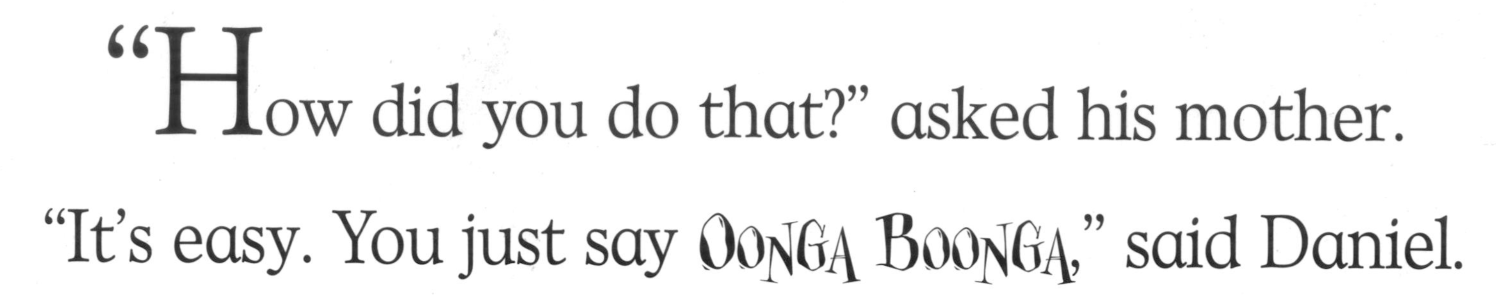

"How did you do that?" asked his mother.

"It's easy. You just say OONGA BOONGA," said Daniel.

"OONGA BOONGA," said his mother.

"OONGA BOONGA," said his father.

"OONGA BOONGA," said Grandma and Grandpa.

"See," said Daniel. "She likes it."

And sure enough, she did.

Louise was smiling from ear to ear.

"OONGA BOONGA,"

said everyone in unison.

"I'm going out to play," said Daniel.

"Be back at six for dinner," said his mother.

But as soon as he left, Louise's smile faded.

Slowly a tear rolled down her cheek, followed by another and then another. And soon she was crying as loudly as before.

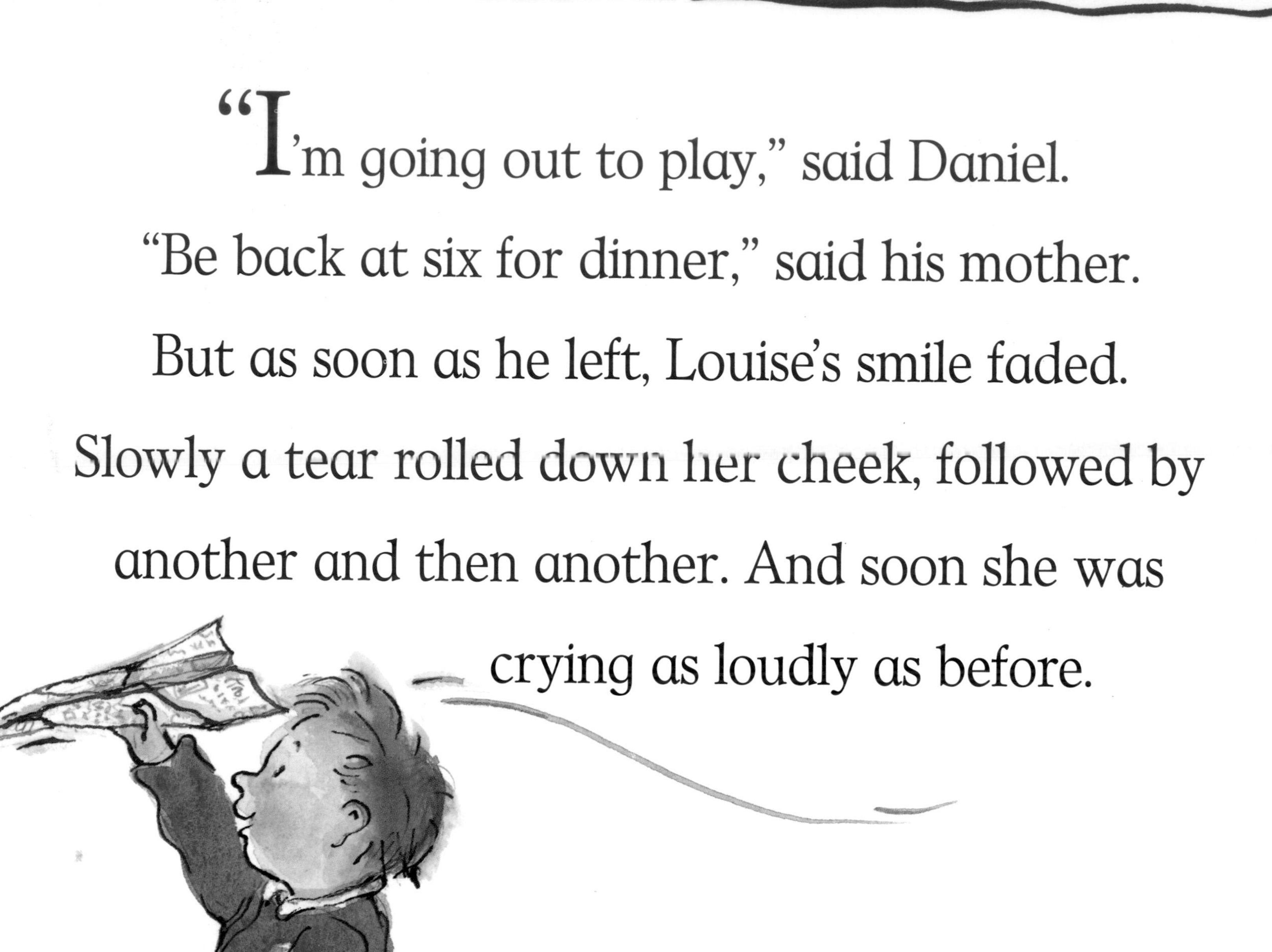

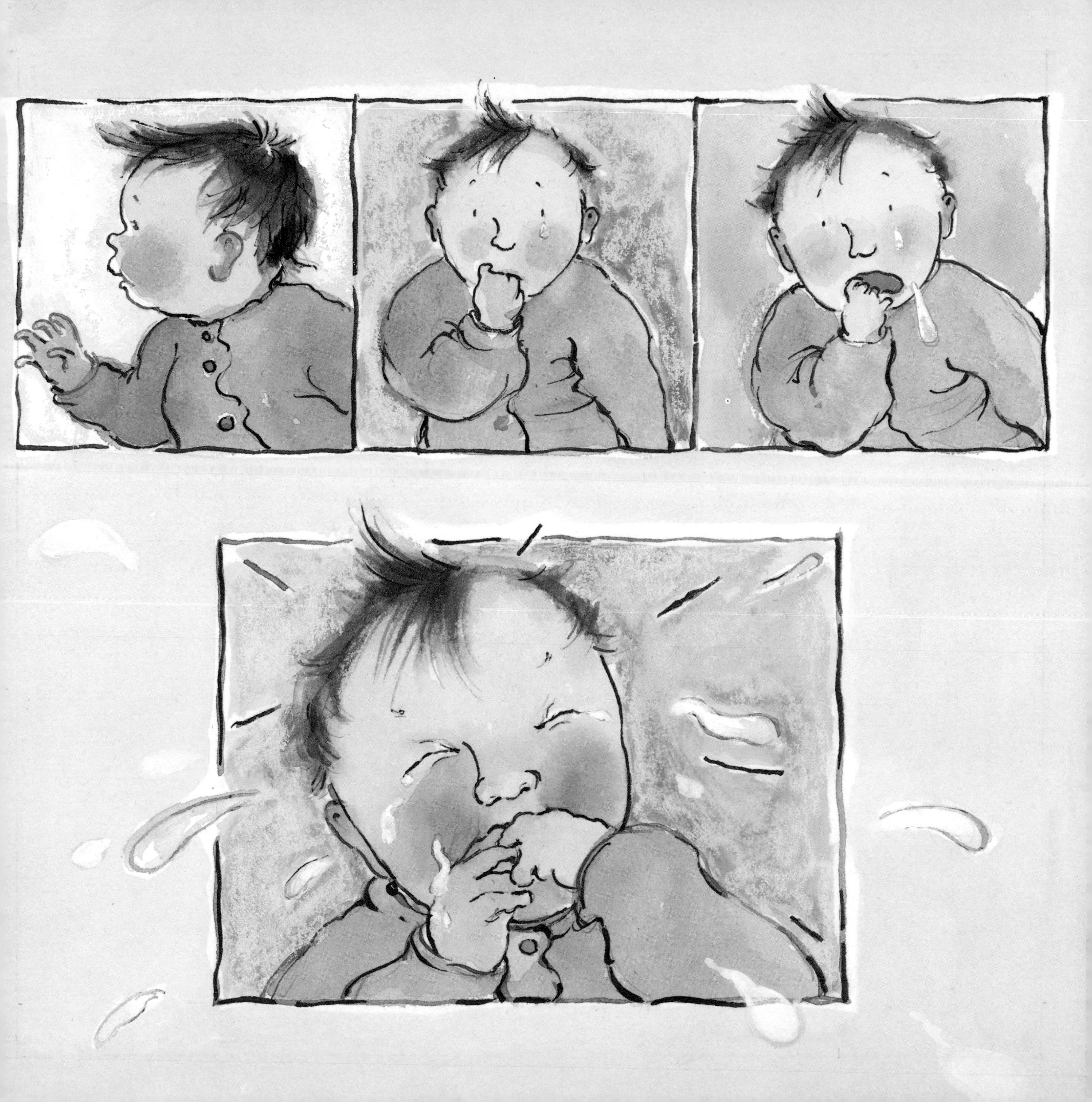

"Oonga Boonga," said her mother.

"Oonga Boonga," said her father.

"Oonga Boonga," said Grandma and Grandpa.

But nothing helped. Louise kept on crying.

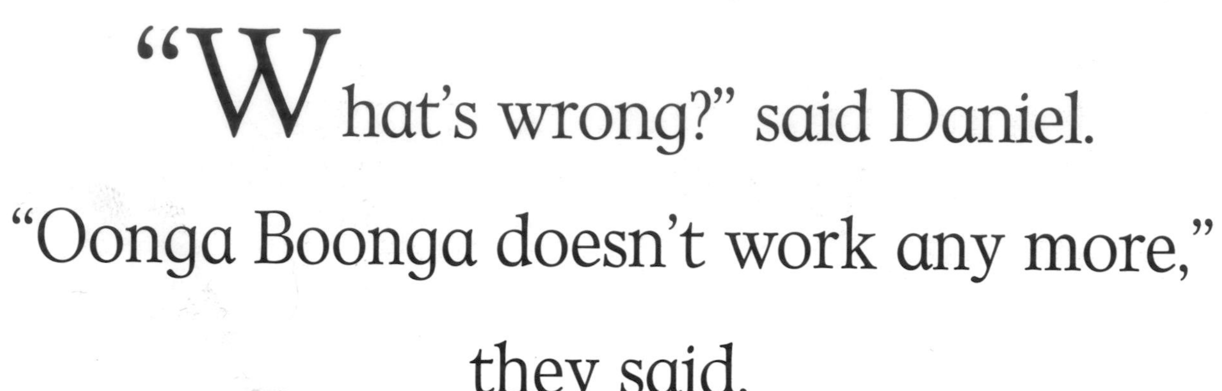

"What's wrong?" said Daniel.

"Oonga Boonga doesn't work any more,"

they said.

Wah
Wah
waah
agh!

Daniel leant over Louise and whispered in her ear:

"BUNKA WUNKA, Louise."

And Louise stopped crying.

Waah